The Survival of Molly Southbourne

ALSO BY TADE THOMPSON

The Murders of Molly Southbourne
Making Wolf

THE WORMWOOD TRILOGY
Rosewater
The Rosewater Insurrection
The Rosewater Redemption

THE SURVIVAL OF
MOLLY SOUTHBOURNE

TADE THOMPSON

A TOM DOHERTY ASSOCIATES BOOK

NEW YORK

This is a work of fiction. All of the characters, organizations, and events portrayed in this novella are either products of the author's imagination or are used fictitiously.

THE SURVIVAL OF MOLLY SOUTHBOURNE

Cover design by Christine Foltzer
Cover art by Wojciech Zwoliński/Arcangel Images

A Tor.com Book
Published by Tom Doherty Associates
120 Broadway
New York, NY 10271

www.tor.com

Tor® is a registered trademark of
Macmillan Publishing Group, LLC.

ISBN 978-1-250-21725-7 (ebook)
ISBN 978-1-250-21726-4 (trade paperback)

First Edition: July 2019

For Maria Adeola

I shall feel the affections of a sensitive
being, and become linked to the
chain of existence and events,
from which I am now excluded.

—**Mary Shelley,** *Frankenstein*

The Survival of Molly Southbourne

One

I am holding a telephone while watching a house burn.

"Please hold," says the voice on the other end of the line.

It is both my house and not, but that will become clearer with time. It is not an accident; this is arson, and were this crime to be investigated, I would be found guilty of it, even though I had nothing to do with the decision to set such a fire. I would be found guilty of using an accelerant, in this case petrol, and piling furniture in a manner that ensures the best blaze. My fingerprints on the can, on all the furniture, my DNA everywhere. An abundance of genetic material, in fact. An investigator paying attention would find more of my blood than it is possible to find from one person.

"Please hold."

The phone receiver is smeared with my blood, as is the Hogarth Avenue sign where I brushed against it on my way here. I'm bleeding from both palms because of my escape through a broken window. I covered the jagged edges in fabric, but it seems the glass cut through. I was so jacked on adrenaline that I didn't feel it. I have cuts on my knuckles from fighting and circular bruises around my wrists and ankles from being chained down. My ribs are bruised and every movement hurts. I slide to the floor of the phone booth, stretching the cord, fielding waves of déjà vu. In typical London fashion, the booth is filthy, but I can't care right now. I'm not clean, anyway. The left arm cuff of my top rides up, and I can see the crude tattoo of the phone number I just called. A new tattoo, redness all around, some dots of blood because it wasn't done well.

The house flares up, triumphant like a Neanderthal's campfire, with flames rising up in the morning breeze, yellow highlights against the blue-black cloud of smoke. Shame. It's a good house. It *was* a good house.

"Hello?" says a harried voice.

"Hello," I say. I don't think my voice sounds as strong as I would like.

"Confirm your name, please?"

"I already did."

"Again, please."

"Molly Southbourne."

"Thank you. Are you injured?"

"Yes, but I think it's minor."

"Are you bleeding?"

"Yes."

"Have you been unconscious?"

"Yes."

"How many?"

"Excuse me?"

"How many of them were there?"

Oh. *Them.* "Five or six."

"All right. Molly, I need you to stay exactly where you are. We need to contain the blood, as I'm sure you know."

"Yes."

"A team will be with you in fifteen minutes. Do not come out of the phone booth and do not speak to anyone."

"What about the police?"

"Especially not the police, Molly. Don't worry. We'll fix whatever happens."

~

They're here in ten minutes, six of them, one in a suit with official papers and ID that makes the police and fire service melt away. Five of them are in protective gear, hazmat or something. They spray me where I stand even before checking my medical condition. They follow my path on Hogarth Avenue, spraying the pavement where they find blood. They incinerate my clothes as a medic attends to my hands and the rest of my body until she is convinced that I no longer leak essential fluids. When the fire is out, they cover the burnt house in a fumigation tent and do whatever it is that they do. I sit in a car and wait. I sort through memories and impressions.

Neighbors have gathered to watch. I know them because Molly knew them. She never interacted, just observed their lives in silence. The lone old man with the suspect video equipment delivery. The pregnant newlyweds to her left. The snooty kid from number fifteen. Murder-cake woman at number eight, suspected to have killed her husband, but not served time for it, likes to bake at Christmas.

The suit comes to speak to me, or rather to interrogate me under the guise of debriefing. I tell him a version of events, enough to allay his suspicions but not enough to expose me.

When we're done he says, "Okay, Molly, we'll get packed up, then take you to your new place in a few minutes. Stay here."

"Okay." I close my eyes and rest my forehead against the cool glass.

The thing is, I'm not Molly Southbourne.

~

Okay, I am, but I'm not the Molly they think I am.

I look, to any observer, like I'm twenty-six, twenty-seven. I'm only about eighteen hours old.

The Molly Southbourne they think I am is dead, her body burned up in the fire. I did not kill her.

Molly Southbourne was a freak whose blood grew genetically identical duplicates of her. One drop of blood, and a new molly popped up, but it wasn't cute. It wanted to kill her. Molly spent her whole life killing her duplicates just to survive, but it was too much for her to deal with emotionally, so she arranged to kill herself.

I am one of the duplicates, the last surviving one, I believe. She made me, beat me into submission, chained me down, told me her story, then gave me the keys to free myself, not caring whether I lived or died, whether I took her identity or not. She set fire to the house, and died fighting other duplicates that she made.

I escaped, and here I am.

These people cleaning up are part of an arrangement Molly's mother made before she died. One phone call, and whatever mess Molly has made gets neutralized. They used to get called in when she was overwhelmed by duplicates and unable to clean up the bloody chaos created in the process of murdering them. That's why Mr. Suit and the rest of them think they are here.

They are treating my spilled blood with chemicals because they think it will grow duplicates. It will not.

Duplicates are sterile.

In my head, I can feel the slow return of Molly's memories. Stories Molly told me just hours ago recur in stereo. It's a weird double image, double sensation.

I hope they don't take me out of London.

~

They find me a place in Acton, a two-bedroom flat on a quiet street. They give me the credentials for a building society account with a warning not to "overdo it."

"Do not, under any circumstances, go back to Hogarth Avenue. Good luck, and be more careful when you bleed." And he is gone.

Molly's rules are stricter:

Don't bleed.

If you see yourself coming, run.

Blot, burn, bleach.

None of this is a risk to me, so I ignore the rules, and I ignore the fitness and hand-to-hand combat that Molly needed for survival since childhood.

Drones have no fear of laying eggs.

All I have to do is keep my head down and my mouth shut; a quiet life, come what may.

That's the key to survival.

Transcript

[Video is blank at first, showing a furnished front room with nondescript furniture and dozens of books both in and out of shelves. Prof. Down (PD) enters the frame from left and sits on a stool.]

PD: Hello, this is Professor Down, first recording. I've decided instead of accepting my fate, I'm going to try something radical. It might not work, but there's no alternative, so I'm going for it.

I was going to use a central line to deliver nutrients straight into my bloodstream, like they do for cancer patients on Total Parenteral Nutrition, but that needs initiating and maintaining. I can't find anyone to do it for me without a reasonable explanation, which I don't have. I could pay a medical student, but when I made overtures they looked at me as if I were a crypto–drug addict.

I'm going to have to eat the food, eat myself into survival. Cut energy use right down, weaponized laziness.

This is strangely exciting, in part because I am transgressing against a lifetime of healthy eating habits.

I'll do what I can.
Permitte divis cetera.
Leave the rest to the gods.
[cut]

Two

I think of Molly, the original, a lot. I dream of her as well.

I dream I *am* her.

I shut and lock the door on the shackled girl, then turn to the mollys, naked, aflame, and enraged, all of them. There is fire and smoke everywhere, and I can feel my throat tightening, but I have a mission. I fight, though not to win, but to provoke. I want them to fight back, as ferocious as mollys can be, focused on me and not the person behind the door. Something pops and glass shards spray the room.

They are on me, hot sizzling flesh, choosing to grapple rather than strike because of the close quarters and abundant obstacles. There is pain, but I cannot shout because of the smoke. With this lack of oxygen, a lung full of the wrong stuff, all I can do is croak. How are they still active? What are they made of? I just want to give up and die.

They bring me down with a clumsy playground maneuver, pushing me over an extended leg, slamming the back of my head on the floor because I didn't tuck my chin in. My left shoulder pops out of the joint, and my belly is on fire. I know I should smell the cooking flesh, but I don't. A face rises, blackened and bald from the fire, and I punch it with my good arm just to keep the dance going. It has the desired effect and the mollys do not flag. They bite and they gouge and they hit me with furniture-derived improvised weapons. I am above it all now, as the fire spreads and the lack of oxygen narcotizes me. . . .

Then I wake and I open the window and remember who I am, and who I am not. There is always traffic in Acton, always a siren or a scream, or the songs of the amorous or drunk, and it reorients me.

The stories Molly told me are as seeds, each one a focal point for the budding and flowering of memory. The stories of Southbourne Farm, of Pile the dog, of Mykhaila and Connor, her parents, become real images and sequences in my mind. The love for her parents and affection for Professor James Down grow to fill some of the emptiness I have, and is counterbalanced with guilt and regret for being responsible for their demise. And death. So much death, a lifetime of it, from childhood. Killing mollys through the decades.

The last thing that comes to me is my own creation. I see the self-cutting and the dripping of blood into a pile of wood, and the waiting as my cells consume the wood and build a body. I see Molly Prime dress me up and then . . . nothing. It confuses me, this viewpoint, but it is one of Molly's last memories before she died. My memory now.

~

Everything is new, and once I learn to endure the pain and nightmares, I enjoy discovering the rest of existence. I walk a lot, taking in the aromatic smells of the kebab shops, feeling the wind on my face, staring at the faces of strangers in crowds, touching the barks of different kinds of trees, examining the different kinds of vomit on Sunday mornings from Londoners' Saturday nights out, considering the weird inconsistencies of the city geography: Acton hosts Hammersmith Hospital, while Hammersmith hosts Charing Cross Hospital. There is no actual hospital at Charing Cross. The pineapples that tip the obelisks on Lambeth Bridge, the weird, incongruously bright Madonna outside the Church of the Precious Blood in Southwark, and the monuments to the disinterred dead whose graves were along the proposed Underground lines. After reading about it in a book, I visit Sir Richard Burton's tomb and see for myself the stone tent at Mortlake.

I stare at clouds. I have them in my memory, but that does not prepare me. I go to the park, lie down, and look at the sky, making shapes.

The record shops and street dancers fascinate me, and I spend time in Shepherds Bush and Ladbroke Grove, stealing fashion bits and pieces here and there till one of the kids says I look like a Buffalo Gal from the 1982 Malcolm McLaren hip-hop song. He means it as a put-down, but I don't care. What is fashion but periodically changing attitudes? What is old will become new again, and the new will become old. So I wear the large ruffled skirts and a variety of hats and masklike eye shadow because I like it. I'll change when I feel like it.

I cut myself and bleed on the carpet, but nothing grows from my blood. The voice in my head most of the time is Mykhaila's, and she explains the duplicates to Molly.

They are not clones or sisters. Best to consider them a kind of fleshy construct, biological robots, androids. Or should that be gyneoids?

So, who programs the robot? Why do they attack? And what is to become of me, now that Molly One is dead?

This existence fills me with an aimlessness. I am constantly waiting to be attacked by mollys, but they never come. The waiting marinates my blood with adrenaline, which makes me anxious and ready for a fight. No duplicates appear, I never see my own self coming toward me.

I go to the farm where I was born, where Molly was born, but nothing remains of the Southbourne family. The house is rubble, the fencing removed, the land reclaimed by vegetation, which surprises me because it was sold, not abandoned.

I go to my old university, clinging to familiarity like ivy to a tree. I do not feel better for doing this, worse when I see James Down, my erstwhile lover. I don't think it's been two months since I, since Molly One, last saw him, yet he has ballooned in size. His clothes are ill-fitting, his cheeks swollen, squeezing his eyes into slits, his skin blotchy with eruptions and diseased. I see him in the quad, stuffing his face, not with hunger but with a compulsive desperation that speaks of addiction. The last time I saw him, he said I had killed him. He seems to be intent on killing himself.

I leave without speaking to him, with a deep feeling of dissatisfaction.

The whole nostalgia business leaves me with an ache, and I pick up a guy to fuck from a jazz place in Hammersmith, but it doesn't feel right. He is unhappy when I tell him to leave, but I insist. I think he's going to hit me, or try to hit me, but he seems to think better of it. Good for him. The mood I'm in, I may have killed him if I had to fight him off. I have a strong hunger, a need to be held by a woman, but I do not know the rules so it takes weeks before I meet someone. This helps still my restless soul for two days, but the yearning returns, that yammering of the mind, that disquiet. I work my way through a number of women in West London, but my ache does not go away, and I get a reputation for not being serious. I cannot find the right femme because I am not the right femme.

I think I'm missing my mother. I spend hours meditating, conjuring up all the memories I have. I do not know her people. She left the country too early, and Mykhaila isn't her real name. I do know my father's people, though. I know of them. They're in Dublin, a place I don't know and have no inclination to visit until I feel safer in my own skin.

I know, from the force of Molly's memory, that I should be going to the gym, to keep my skills sharp and my body ready, but ready for what? I don't have duplicates; there is no danger of waking up with my double trying to strangle me. I do not need to be the strongest or the fastest, neither do I need to be fastidious in the disposal of blood.

I wander about London, adrift, sometimes lost in a cannabinoid haze. I pass HMP Wormwood Scrubs, notorious prison, former dueling ground in the 1800s. I run through the open fields, trying to catch some of the care-free attitude of my childhood, of Molly's childhood, and failing.

I don't know exactly when I get lost, but I stop at some point. While I am no longer running, my thoughts are. I cannot stop thinking, and the people are staring at me, and I think they can hear what I'm thinking, which makes me want to stop thinking, but I can't and it's frightening. Am I running yet? No. I'm out of the grass, onto the street, and people are staring, wanting to kill me. I run from them. Some man tries to hold me down, to bury me in the asphalt, so I break his arm. I am gentle, although his screams suggest otherwise. Believe me, not him.

The police arrive, for me, to lock me up, no doubt. I dispatch the two officers quickly. They can call backup to look after them, because feeling the way I do, I don't want to deal with people anymore. I have never been so terrified, and I can no longer hear my mother's voice in my head.

Everybody I pass is staring at me. Each person in the shop fronts, every face in every magazine, all the drivers of all the cars, all the bicycle messengers, the beautiful faces on the billboards, all snap their heads in my direction and they do not blink. I feel like prey, so I run faster. Mostly, people part, but some are in my way, and I take them down with prejudice. Why are they all after me? What do they know? I need a place to hide so I can figure things out. Blue lights flashing, a meat wagon cutting me off. Police, in riot gear, no guns that I can see, six of them, self-confident, clubs drawn.

"Lie down on the pavement! Lie down right now! Do it!"

No.

I weave, and though I try to avoid them, I run smack into their scrum. So be it. I'll take as many of them with me as possible. Some people are screaming. When a truncheon hits me in the mouth and one of the voices stops, I realize I was one of the screaming ones all along.

When you are fighting multiple opponents your aim is not to beat them. Your aim is to escape, so you fight in one direction, to thin a barrier, to form a hole, and to run through it.

You can't break a police truncheon with a karate chop, but if you strike it hard enough in the right spot, and the strap is wrapped around the officer's hand, you can break the wrist. I do this. The muffled scream creates a delay when the other five think of helping.

Don't hit the armor.

I aim for the points of articulation, just below the vest, the necks, the shoulders—it's not working. I am too tired, too fatigued, or my strategy is not correct for the situation. Truncheons hit me with precision—the officers do not obstruct one another like amateurs would. Flashes of light and pain.

Change strategy—harm minimization.
I can't escape, but I can curl up into a ball.
Pain.
Oh, Mother, what pain.

~

A month later I'm in hell.

I'm in a hospital, under a section of the Mental Health Act, on medication, fat and sluggish, but no longer paranoid. It's not what you think. There is no Nurse Ratched, no beatings, no cold showers, no compulsory group therapy, no cuckoo, no nest, and no one flying over anything. There are still daily humiliations. There is still shock treatment, though not for everybody. Nobody has come for me. I am allowed phone calls, but only if I tell them who I am calling. I have not told them my name, and I refuse to give an alias. They are literally calling me Jane Bloggs. They tell me when to eat and when to shower and when to go to bed. The coffee is decaf and the water is always lukewarm. The tea is always weak because we are not allowed boiling water. The day is predictable. They call you for breakfast, they herd you to groups, they herd you to ward rounds, they herd you to the dispensary for medication, they herd you back to other groups, then you get evening meds and free time, which is always used for TV because you can't be arsed to do anything else.

My brain is shrunken, trapped in a larger sluggish brain surrounding the core of me. This is not my body, but also is. This never happened to Molly One. This body is uniquely mine. There are others in here with me, but it is not for me to tell their stories. I like some of them and detest others. The old me could escape from this place, but the new me is too slow. I shouldn't have detested James's size. I'm like him now, with an appetite so ravenous it seems to be separate and alive in its own right.

"You've had a psychotic break," says the psychiatrist. "You went berserk in Shepherds Bush and injured seventeen people, five of them hospitalized. We found cannabis in your urine. Did you take any other drugs?"

Silence.

"If you talk to me, I can help."

Silence.

"Do you have family?"

I yawn, but inside I picture my mother and father, two mutilated corpses on Southbourne Farm, the work of a molly. Not a story I intend to tell my captors.

This is a weekly occurrence. There are three ways out of here. One is to escape, two is to make a phone call, and three is to play the game, tell them what they think they want to hear and escape. No, wait. That doesn't make sense. Three is to be discharged as healed.

I do have strange beliefs that I don't talk about. I think some of the mollys are still alive, the last ones from Hogarth, wandering around, untethered from society, looking for me. I imagine they look like the living dead, shriveled, burned up, contracted, moving with insect-like jerkiness. I lose certainty about who I am, and I start to think of myself as the first Molly.

I don't think I can fight well the way I am, soft muscles, layers of fat, breathing heavy just climbing stairs, swollen feet that I can barely see.

Worse, I can't formulate a plan. I try to think and the ideas stick together for seconds, then disintegrate in my mind. I don't remember them, I just remember that there is something I've forgotten. If I write things down, I risk being discovered when these cunts go into my room. And that's not paranoia; they do, and they don't even try to hide it.

Okay, new plan: Have to stop the medication from getting in me. Pretend to swallow, regurgitate in the room, that's the way. The next dosing time I try it, but I'm caught, and they inject me for like a week before going back to tablets.

"Rookie mistake," says Gen, an inmate I talk to. She's in a wheelchair, and has been there for two years. "You don't swallow and vomit. You pretend to swallow."

She holds her hand out, palm up, and moves her other

hand over it, and a pill appears. She swallows this with a flourish. I watch her gullet bob up and down her neck, then she opens her mouth and raises her tongue. Then she strokes my cheek and the tablet falls to the ground.

"You practice."

She shows me how. I don't attempt it until she says I'm ready. It is the only thing I can consistently keep in my head, even when I'm fucking Gen in her wheelchair weeks later. I feel nothing, just copulating out of habit, or boredom. Prestidigitation is more interesting and important. I do it well, and after two weeks of stopping my medication, my mind is clearer.

"I'd like to stab Jesus," says Gen, one night in her room.

"Why?" I say. "What did he ever do to you?"

"Nothing. I just want to cut him so I can drink his blood. I've always wondered what kind of wine it would be."

"He didn't have wine for blood, Gen. He turned water into wine."

She considers this. "Communion."

"That's metaphorical."

"Not according to the Vatican. Either way, I'd take him to a waterfall and tell him to transform it into wine."

Gen is unobtrusive, has a minor obsession with Madame Blavatsky and magic in general, but she surprises me in the end.

"I called that number on your arm," she says.

We're in her room after lights-out, and I sit up. "What?"

"I was curious." Her voice is so low, it almost doesn't register.

"You shouldn't have done that, Gen."

"I know. I'm sorry."

"What happened?"

"Nothing. I heard a few clicks, a hiss, then silence. I said, 'Hello?' and a voice said, 'Name?' so I said mine without thinking. The line went dead. That's it."

"When was this?" I'm dressing up now.

"Two days ago."

"Two . . . Gen, fuck, why didn't you tell me?"

I don't listen to the explanation. I'm out and back in my own room, thinking of what this means. There's a moon, a new one, and I stare at it like some tainted celestial oracle. I don't know if my number is unique to me, or what Gen's name and voice would mean to a person on the other end. Something crinkles in my pocket, a piece of paper, folded. It's a crude plan of the unit, with points requiring a pass indicated. Gen probably made this and slipped it in while I wasn't looking.

The next day I just walk out of the unit.

I'm surprised at how easy it is. There's a Walking Group who have permission to leave the unit. I insinuate myself into it and lift the pass of one of the staff members, and, using Gen's map, I let myself out.

First phone booth I come to I call my emergency number collect.

"Name?"

"Molly Southbourne," I say.

There's a brief delay on the other end. "Hang tight, allow them to recapture you. Do not resist. We'll be there in a few hours. Have you bled?"

"No."

"Have you killed anyone?"

"No."

"Good. Don't."

~

In a few hours I'm a free woman, but only in my mind. I am restricted by this body that is a consequence of medication and my mental illness. Molly One was never overweight, and neither was our mother. My mother. Her mother.

I call the hospital, ask to speak to Gen, but she won't take the call. I recall the last time we spoke. "I think you made me pregnant that time," she told me one day after sex. I asked her to explain but she went off on a tangent, as she was prone to.

I walk first, all over London. I still have my anatomy knowledge and running at my weight might be hell on my joints. I do what I'm meant to. I cut calories, bump my protein, I start to work out again, I graduate to running.

Running is good, and once I get over the creaky joints, the split shins, and the lactic acid muscle damage, a rhythm develops during which I can think. And I get to thinking about my father, about Connor Southbourne, and I think of where he's from, and how I'd like to have some family.

About that time, I'm pretty sure I'm being watched, and not the paranoid kind.

Transcript

Vomiting. Lots of it.

My body clearly isn't ready for the onslaught of nutrition. I'm nauseated all the time now, but I have to push on.

[cut]

Diarrhea now.

I have . . . Excuse me.

[PD exits hastily from the screen. Sounds of flatulence heard in background.]

[cut]

All right. Metoclopramide in high doses works for the nausea. I'll have to wait the diarrhea out because I want the food to be absorbed. I'm already 10 kilos heavier. That's like three very small babies.

I need to slow my metabolism. I've started carbimazole in an attempt to inhibit my thyroid gland. The only risk is hypothyroidism, which might affect my thinking.

Eh. Thinking is overrated anyway.

[cut]

Three

I wake, escaping from a dream of moistness and James Down. Not a sexy dream, but not a frightening one either. I can't remember what happened in it, but I did not want to be there. I go for a walk while it's still dark, although the drunks are out. Not too many other people, but at least the cold air cuts through the fog of the dream. I'm fully alert and awake when I get the sense that I'm being followed.

It has been quiet, the kind of quiet that makes you think the danger has passed, the kind that makes you go soft, less vigilant.

I do not even know that I know how to spot someone following me until it happens. Instincts bubble to the surface and long-dormant spycraft comes into focus. It feels like my body is being driven by another consciousness. This possession helps me use reflective surfaces, to double back on myself on the bridge at White City, to pretend casualness, and to clock all of them.

When my conscious mind tries to assert itself, I feel confusion and indecision, and as such, I stay loose, submerge myself, let instincts take over.

After fifteen minutes, I no longer sense them. Confused, I wonder if I imagined the surveillance in the first place. I make my way back to the flat, where, despite my imaginings, my movie notions of importance, nobody has tossed my property or rifled through my documents. I look under the bed to be sure nobody is there. I always do this. I remember one savage evening returning to a dorm room and finding a molly under the bed. There is none.

I make tea with the meager supplies. It tastes like the bag is from 1979. TV on, boots and hat off, tea in hand, I watch the Berlin Wall come down. The GDR's *Antifascistischer Schutzwall,* the news analysts tell me, is a symbol of the Cold War, the collapse a metaphor for the victory of democracy and capitalism over communism, which is dead. I notice they do not speak of Red China. Tiananmen Square is still fresh in my memory, particularly that one protester staring down tanks. Twenty-four-hour news is a boon for insomniacs everywhere, but it wearies my soul, or it would if I had one.

When it is proper morning I leave the flat and retrace my steps westward. I see nobody following me. I spot a goldcrest on the concrete barrier, tiny, grooming, then gone in a flash of yellow. I eat at a greasy spoon and watch hordes of students and tourists materialize as the morning wears on, feeling apprehension in my gut. When I feel the hairs on my neck rise, I know for sure. I recognize the face of the woman who just arrived, but not from where. I may have seen her while passively scanning the crowds. She's black, not very tall, walks with brisk, powerful strides, short hair, about old enough to be a mature student, but I see something in her movements and her flickering gaze, and the way she does not look at me. My whole Buffalo Gal persona is there for a reason. Most people stare at me, so the ones not paying attention are usually the ones who are studying me. Usually.

I get up and go to the toilet, mostly to think, but just as I close the door, I peer through the gap. I see that she has stood and seems to be coming after me. She moves like a killer robot from a movie, although when we get killer robots I'm sure they won't be humanoid.

There are two stalls, both empty. There's a sink that suffers from incomplete cleaning, with a grimy mirror in which my reflection has wide eyes, but why? Fear? Excitement? Anticipation? I take off my jacket and one boot. I lay the jacket over the mirror to muffle the sound, then smash it with the boot heel. The shards fall into the sink and I select a long thin one as I hear the steps come to a stop at the door. I leave the jacket over the sink and enter the furthermost stall as the door opens. In silence, I undo my bandanna and wrap it around the shard, leaving two inches exposed as a blade. My hair tumbles free, but I can live with that. The woman opens the first stall, does not go in.

I wait, she waits. I hold my breath. Water drips somewhere.

At once, shock, the sound of the door and the silence splintering in the middle. I know I've been shot, no pain, but warm wetness along my side, and a bland throbbing from far away, as if outside my body.

Don't bleed.

Fuck this.

I launch myself at the door, ignoring the new lancing in my flank. I slip on some water, but this takes me barreling into my attacker, sending us both to the floor. She shoots again, or at least tries to. The empty click of a misfire. I'm on top of her, holding her gun wrist with my left hand. Before she can react I stab her in the forearm and drag the shard up, widening the wound toward the elbow. She flings me off her, but the gun falls. I expect this move and I roll to my feet, into a crouch. She rises, her right hand droopy because I've severed tendon and nerve, blood dripping to the tiles and pooling.

Don't bleed.

There are urgent knocks at the door, but this woman is unflappable. Her eyes flick to the gun, then back to me. She seems to have jammed it, but I don't know how and

I'm not going to risk looking.

"I don't mean you any harm, Molly."

Sometimes an enemy will say something to disarm or discombobulate you during a fight, dorogoy. There is a time to listen, but during a fight is not it. Ignore everything, even if the person speaks of surrender. The time to surrender is before the fight. Once you start combat, finish it.

I don't answer. I close the distance and she tries clumsily to defend herself. I kick her left shin with my booted foot, I slap her wounded arm, a feint that opens her neck to me. I smack her with all I have right where the trachea meets the lower jaw. She goes limp as I fall to my knees. I'm dizzy from blood loss, but I drag myself to the gun, release the chambered round, chamber it again, then crawl into the toilet stall, aiming it at the door. If anyone else is coming after her, I'll—

I faint.

Transcript

No, that's not the only risk of antihistamines. Fucking urticarial rash. I look like an improperly cooked lobster.

But, hey, antihistamines cause weight gain.

[cut]

I thought about Molly today. I drove past her house, but it's a ruin. I couldn't find anyone who knew what had happened to her, but they said nobody died in the fire.

[cut]

Four

I have to go to hospital again, even though I hate it and protest when I come round. I have to have a laparotomy and so on to get blood and shit out of my abdomen and join my bowels back together again. I have a colostomy at some point, but they fix it back. I get a blood transfusion. I heal.

The people at the end of my number fix it with the police, but they interrogate me as soon as I'm back home. The guy in the suit, same as before, asks all the questions.

"What did you do to provoke her?"

Nothing.

"Had you met her before?"

No.

"Why did you kill her?"

I was defending myself.

"How did you get injured?"

I'm out of shape.

"Did she say anything?"

She said she didn't mean me any harm.

"Are you lying to me?"

No.

"Tell me again what you did to provoke her."

It goes on for two hours.

Afterward, he says I'm idle and should get a job. "If you keep your mind busy, you'll stay out of trouble."

Right. It is my idle mind that made her bring the gun.

~

I do get a job, though.

Assistant in the pathology section of Central Middlesex Hospital. I prepare sections of breast biopsies for the histopathologists. It is repetitive, precise work, and I take to it rapidly. Within a fortnight, my life has some rhythm, spending nine to five during the week at work, then reading at the Hammersmith Library in the evenings. I spend Fridays at the record shops and hang out with the b-boys of Shepherds Bush. I passively start to look for a martial arts club, because Molly's routines are starting to assert themselves in me, and it feels odd not to train regularly.

Loneliness is a heavy weight that constantly tries to drag me into despair. I think of James a lot and I almost phone him a number of times. I don't yearn for him romantically, I just miss talking to someone who can keep up with me. I'm musing on this when I hear a sound in the bathroom. I'm still complacent, I guess, because

I think it's something benign, like my toothbrush falling over. It's not, and I'm unprepared for what I see when I check.

It's a naked molly.

If you see yourself, run.

I back away. Why is there a molly? Where is it from? When did I bleed?

Its eyes follow me, locked on like a heat-seeking missile. Then it launches at me, arms raised, hands clawed, mouth open as if it's going to bite me. I flinch, and cringe, cowed in the moment, eyes squeezed shut, waiting for the attack, but it does not come. I open my eyes and there is nothing there.

I sweep through the whole flat, both rooms, the bathroom (again), corridor, kitchen, and look out of all the windows. Nothing. Not even cats or urban foxes stir. No barn owls fly, no insects chirp. No sirens, even. London asleep.

Oh, sweet holy fuck, I'm seeing things. I don't have enough enemies, so I have to invent them.

~

The thing is, I have a history of psychosis dating back to childhood. Molly does. After my release from the mental hospital, they gave me pills, which I did not take. Probably not the best move. This feels different, though. I've never seen things, and I don't feel that creeping paranoia, that restlessness, that impending doom, that goes with my breakdowns. I do not feel mad.

I decide to start taking my pills again. That'll sort it out.

~

It doesn't. I keep seeing mollys, standing in the rain among a crowd of people waiting for a bus, behind the counter at a deli untouched by the other waiting staff, on the television squeezed between the newscasters, among the crops on the allotment outside my window, floating above my bed after midnight, waiting on a zebra crossing while I pass in a bus, always staring and tracking me.

These mollys are different from the kind Molly Prime used to encounter. For one thing, other than the first, they are not violent. They are usually expressionless or look disappointed in me. There is, I suppose, no overt hostility, even though I expect it. I wait, and after fifteen or twenty minutes, they disappear. Except one time when a molly followed me onto the tube and stayed with me for two hours. I have tried to touch them. For a time this was impossible, as they avoided me when I came near, but they apparently cannot read my mind, because

I faked motion in one direction and caught one in the other. She wisps out of my hands. Until that moment I wasn't sure whether they were solid or not. I am sure that nobody else can see them.

I suppose I killed enough mollys to warrant a haunting, but I don't believe in ghosts, and I hate problems that I cannot punch into submission.

After three weeks of this, I'm on edge. I wonder if I'm being given a message by my body. One day I grab a knife and cut my forearm lightly, but enough to draw blood. I let it drip to the floor and wait. Ten minutes, half an hour, two hours, and nothing happens to the blood except drying and flaking. I wake up every few minutes and check on it, but no growth. For the next week I cut myself every night and don't follow the blot, bleach, burn rules that rattle around in my skull from my Prime.

I am still sterile. My blood does not grow mollys, but my mind does. Ultimately, I grow used to these ghosts, I become less alarmed, and with time I learn to ignore them. They still have the most alarming wide-eyed stares, but I become adept at subtracting them from my visual field, and life continues.

Five

I should have known that I was under some kind of surveillance, because I get a phone call from the cleanup people for the first time a few days after I start taking the medication. They call me at work, during my lunch break, which is considerate, I suppose.

"We want you to come in for some tests." He gives an address on Uxbridge Road close to Ealing Broadway.

"This is not . . . I'm working."

"Leave for the day. Say you are sick, Molly."

Click. Hangs up.

I rack my brain and memory, such that it is. I have no recollection of these people ever calling Molly. They are responsive, antibodies that show up when something is awry. They have no reason to activate now, unless I am showing signs of something being wrong and I can't see it.

Am I going in to meet with them? No. For one thing, I hate being told what to do. More important is what they will probably do to me. The tests they want to run may not be purely psychological, if I'm reading the situation right, which means they are likely to find out that I'm *a* molly, not *the* Molly.

I am, as the Americans say, getting the hell out of Dodge.

~

I have at most thirty minutes, maybe forty, before they realize I'm not on the way to them. I have the taxi park on double yellow lines and leave the engine running because I want to be able to leave quickly. As I rush up the stairs, I realize I have no plan, no allies, no bolt-hole.

The key is in my lock when I hear footsteps from down the corridor. It's dark in that direction, overhead lights out. I see her coming, but when she steps into the light I'm taken aback, but only for a second. It's her. The woman I killed before. Or, am I seeing things? Like I've been seeing mollys?

"Molly"—she shows me her hands, empty—"I mean you no harm."

"You said that the last time," I say. "Who are you?" I'm not interested in the answer. I'm edging closer to get her within striking distance.

There is no such thing as fighting dirty or fighting fair. These are categories for the weak, or the unfit. Your sole purpose is to survive, which you will do by winning each conflict, every time. You use everything in your environment, you use every body part you can muster to your purpose, you break every oath, disappoint every friend, throw sand in every eye, but you win, and you walk away. Let those play actors in the sports arena worry about rules.

The mollys I see don't talk to me. They don't stick around. I blink, look away, then back, but she is still there. Should I warn her off? My mother says no, my mother says attack and kill.

"My name is Tamara and I just want to talk," she says. Her hair is tied in an African print scarf.

I nod. She's wearing an open coat, might be a weapon in there. Her eyes flicker away from mine for an instant, and I know there's someone behind me before I hear the footfalls. I resist the natural instinct to turn. I punch Tamara in the center of her face, crushing her nose, almost lifting her off her feet. She makes no sound as she falls. I turn, and am surprised to see another Tamara coming at me, but this does not make me hesitate. She has learned some basic hand-to-hand skills somewhere, but she's not very good. Karate, I think. I avoid her strikes easily, grab her right arm, turn my back into her, and fling her over my shoulder. While she's winded on the floor I kick her head until she's out. I'm breathing heavy and my knuckles hurt. I'm out of condition, or I never was in the condition Molly Prime was in, and where her hands were

53

callused mine are smooth from soft living.

I search both the tamaras, find one small gun between them, the kind of .22 you slip into a handbag. I drop it in the cavernous pockets of my ruffled skirt. I can hear thumps, getting louder, like people running toward me. I get into my flat and take a few seconds to look around, knowing I'll never see it again. I catch myself in the mirror, eye shadow running down my face from the sweat. I look like a sad clown.

I wish I had time to pack.

I smash an occasional table and pick up one of the legs just as the door breaks inward and three tamaras charge in. I go low for the first, whacking my improvised club against her kneecaps. She goes sprawling, and smashes her chin on the ground. The second grabs my club-hand, just as I intended. I kick her in the crotch, then bodily lift her and slam her into the third.

There are more. I fight, I win.

There are more still, jostling for the chance to get to me.

I fight, I win.

More still. I shoot the gun until it's empty.

More.

Then it's all pain and blackness.

Transcript

Clothes. Need new clothes. I can't fit into any of my trousers and my jackets are impossible to wear. T-shirts and slack-waists is what I need. Think elasticated, XXL.

I can feel the cold where the mass is growing. This must be what Leon felt, the poor sod. Maybe this is how I'll go: cold spreading itself from my core until the rest of me joins it and my heart stops, followed by my brain.

I mustn't dwell on that.

These days I focus on crushing my pills, dissolving them in water, and forcing them to stay down. I can't tolerate solid medicine anymore. And look at this.

[PD rolls up sleeve and shows skin to camera. Unclear what he intends to demonstrate because of poor lighting of the scene.]

Jaundice.

My liver is packing up.

Not a good sign at all.

[cut]

Six

My short life has been full of pain and darkness. I grow weary of it.

As light comes back: Tamara.

Tamara is like me, or rather, like Molly Southbourne. She has duplicates, scores of them. She is different in that she does not appear to have killed any of her duplicates, and they don't seem to be hostile to her either.

I awake in a house with all the tamaras, and there is no violence unless I initiate it.

It's a converted church, deconsecrated. The windows I wake to are not stained glass, but they are arched and elaborately worked.

"Don't be afraid, Molly, we are not here to harm you," says one of the tamaras.

To be fair, they have consistently said this. It's finally sinking into my head that they mean what they say. I am tired of punching them, tired of fracturing their skulls and biting their ears off.

The room is pleasant in many ways. The bed is comfortable, with soft pillows, clean, fragrant bedding, and an electric blanket. The room is warm. There are cut flowers in a vase on a desk by the window. There are no paintings on the walls, but the wallpaper is a repeating motif of leaves, petals, and curling vines that I find soothing. Which makes me suspicious.

"Is this real, or am I dreaming?" I ask. Which is silly, because what would she tell me if I were dreaming?

"Everything will become clear, Molly," says the tamara.

"Where's your Prime?"

"'Prime'?"

"The original. Tamara. Where is she?"

"Downstairs. She is very keen to speak to you."

"Good, because I am very keen to speak to her. Where do I find her?"

"She'll find you."

I leave the room into a corridor that is on the second floor, with rails that look down on an open area that would have been the nave of the church, but is now a day area. There are tamaras everywhere. Some are plaiting each other's hair, others studying, one dancing with a Walkman attached to her ears, a few playing chess, all dressed differently, with different haircuts. Do they all live together in harmony, with a Coke and a smile? I have a picture in my mind of a queen bee, a tamara with a gigantic swollen sac that is constantly pushing out tamaras.

I imagine the kind of free-for-all that would result if I had as many mollys in this space.

Every tamara that I pass greets me, from a formal "Good morning" to a nod or raised eyebrow and a "Hi." One asks if I'm hungry. I am pointed toward the bathroom and spare tampons. This level of civility is not what I'm used to from a kidnapper.

When I see Tamara, she's dusting a framed print, and it's obvious that she's the original. Maybe it's a body language thing, maybe it's because she comes right for me with a broad smile, but I know before she opens her mouth.

"Molly Southbourne, it's a pleasure to finally meet you," she says. "I'd offer my hand, but it's a bit dusty. I'm Tamara Koleosho. Do you like the picture?"

It's a black-and-white photograph of a young black man in a suit sitting on a stool and leaning on a coffin. The background suggests he's on a ship. "Seems a little macabre and sad," I say.

"It's even sadder than it seems. That's Jacob Wainwright in 1874. He was a freedman who brought David Livingstone's corpse back to the U.K. This is a photo of him arriving at Southampton. It is said that people marveled at how refined and educated Jacob was, and wanted to extend friendship to African countries as a result. Thanks to Belgium, it didn't quite work out that way." She uses the duster one final time and turns back to me. "Don't worry, you're safe here."

"From what? Kidnapping?" I ask.

"Ahh. I'm sorry about that." She puts her hands out in front of her, open palms. "I want you to know that you are free to leave. If you want money for a taxi to take you home, or if you want one of us to drive you, that's fine. All I ask for now is that you either listen to me or ask me questions so that you can understand the situation. You don't have to, but it's for your own good."

"What's in it for you?"

"Can we come back to that after I've explained?"

Her voice is rich, deep, and friendly. I can't believe she was the same person who attacked me. She's not, obviously. She's wearing a loose maroon blouse and deep blue jeans. Her feet are bare and she smells of cinnamon or nutmeg, something like that. I always mix the two up. She indicates that I should sit on the divan.

"Where's that name from? Koleosho?" I ask, mangling the pronunciation.

She laughs. "Ko-le-o-sho. It's Yoruba. It means 'one who builds houses for wizards' or near enough."

I stare at her.

"You're angry. You're still angry that we had to subdue you to get you here, and to keep you until you calmed down," says Tamara. "Let me apologize again."

"Tamara," I say, "who are you and what do you want with me?"

"I'm like you," she says. "When I bleed, duplicates grow. You can see them all around the house. It's an amazing gift."

Gift? Is she high?

She tells me her mother was Nigerian. As part of shoe-wielding Nikita Khrushchev's Cold War attempts to create a bloc of socialist states on the continent, the Soviet Union started offering university scholarships to black African nationals in the 1960s, an attempt to win minds newly independent from Western colonial influence. This was one of their most subtle programs, the others being to provide matériel, advisers, and logistics for armed insurrection, with Angola being the quintessence. Tamara's mother was one of those selected and sent to Russia.

"I don't know if she volunteered or was coerced or tricked, but she was experimented on, with no obvious adverse effects. She left Russia with a petrochemical engineering degree and returned to Nigeria for a couple of years before moving to London for postgraduate studies, met my dad, and before you know it, bam! Me." She seems tickled by this.

"So you don't know what happened to her in Russia?" I ask. *Or to my own mother. Molly's mother.*

"No," she says. "But I know somebody who does."

"Your copies. How do you get them to behave?" I ask.

Tamara answers cheerfully, "We all have a common goal, which is to survive."

"So you train them? Break them?"

"The duplicates? They're not horses, Molly, why would I break them?"

"Don't they . . . attack and try to kill you where they're made?" I'm getting irritable now, because I think she's playing with me.

She stops, stands, and looks me in the eye. "Do yours?"

"Don't you have a number? Who do you call for . . . cleanup?"

"I don't understand your question, Molly."

I show her my tattoo. "This is the number I call. For help. When . . . the bodies . . ."

"Who picks up the phone when you do this?"

"I don't know. I think they're some kind of government agency. But they're trying to help, to keep things secret when we . . . when you defend yourself from the duplicates."

"Why would you . . . oh. Oh, Molly. Did you kill your duplicates?"

"That's what my mother . . . that's what . . . yes." Something dawns on me just as the opposite dawns on her.

"I don't kill my duplicates, Molly. And they don't attack me. But there are people who are trying to kill us, and they sound suspiciously like the people you've been working with."

~

Imagine if everything you have done all your life was unnecessary. Imagine if you were told right now that breathing is not needed for survival, that nobody else, no other human, bothers to breathe.

Tamara tells me there is a kill squad, and they exterminate duplicates and leave the primes. All her life, Molly, my Prime, had been doing their job for them, living by a code that ensured her duplicates would be efficiently liquidated. The squad just had to keep track of her, and she even did that for them by phoning them.

How could Molly have been so wrong? How could Mykhaila and Connor have taught me this? Why were my duplicates the only homicidal ones? What does this group want with the primes? I remember them asking me to come in, and I shudder.

When I can think again, I realize that Tamara is afraid of me. They all are. The duplicates have stopped moving at random and are paying more attention, responding to my anxiety. I make a judgment.

"I'm not Molly Southbourne," I say. "I'm a duplicate."

Tamara does not react, not visibly. "Where's your original?"

"She killed herself. She could no longer take the constant slaughter." I give her a précis of my own story.

She looks down for a moment, trying to process it all. "So you've never killed a duplicate yourself. You're not at fault."

"I have. I remember every broken neck, every stabbing, every final breath. All those memories are in me, Tamara. I might as well have done it myself."

Three tamaras draw near, defensive.

"It's okay," says Tamara. "It's okay. She's fine."

"I'm not fine," I say.

"She isn't going to hurt me."

The tamaras take steps back, but remain in positions close by.

"I think you need to meet Vitali," says Tamara.

"Who's Vitali?"

"Vitali Ignatiy Nikitovich. Older than God and knows more about us than anyone on the planet. He's the reason I knew about you and the kill squad. He found me, I found you." She turns to the tamara closest to her. "Please get her some appropriate clothes. We're going out."

Seven

We drive for two hours in the night, not stopping for petrol, food, or full bladders.

I like Vitali Ignatiy on sight. He has a beard shot through with grey, a hairline that is halfway across his crown, thick-framed glasses, eyes that are an afterthought—beads pushed into his skull. He has a white T-shirt and a denim jacket on. His belly pushes out pleasantly, like a plush toy. I find him unthreatening.

I hear noises from beneath the floor and I look down.

"Basement. I have a printing press," he says. "You are so much like your mother."

I first think he means my original, then I relax. I don't speak. I run my eyes over his space. Disorganized, but clean. Books and papers all over, pens, glasses of water, mismatched slippers, two lamps, a desk where his hairy forearms rest. There is a photo of him, younger, slimmer, smiling at some woman with surf in the background. The study has a lingering smell of synthetic pine, like he's cleaned up in a hurry for impending company, unexpected but welcome. I think there are cat hairs, but I cannot be sure. There is a radio of some kind, no labeled stations, no real dial I can see, but on, and giving off the hiss of absent stations.

He seems to suddenly become aware of the tamaras. "Thank you, Tamara. I'll take things from here."

When we are alone he gets up and roots about for some handwritten notes, different papers with different levels of oxidation, gathered over time. "Would you like a drink?"

I shake my head. "I try not to indulge. I got lost in drugs one time."

He nods like this is natural. He hands me a photograph. Black and white, a woman, very young, dark hair, looks out from between two men in khakis who are taller than her and whose heads are cut out of the frame. She is in fatigues, but has a smile and bright, intelligent eyes. It's outside on grass and a cloudy day. I see my face in hers.

"Mykhaila," I say. My mouth is dry and I want to take him up on that drink.

"She was sixteen in that photo, and she was not Mykhaila. Not yet."

I touch her face across the years.

"You can call her 'Mother,' you know. She is still in you."

"I know."

"Her name was Michelle White, and she was the

bravest person I've ever known."

"You knew her?" I did not know that she had another name.

He looks uncomfortable.

"Thank you for showing me this, Vitali Ignatiy."

He waves this off. "A week after this photo was taken she was in West Germany and behind the Iron Curtain. She had commando training, and the best of the West poured the knowledge from both sides of the Atlantic into her head. She was fantastic. All her instructors found her charming and incisive, absorbing craft faster than any they had taught before."

I stalk his bookshelves because to be still is to soak up too much of the emotion lacing his words. The titles are in Russian, French, something that might be Turkish.

This story, my mother, the whole thing is important to Vitali Ignatiy. Who is he?

"Your mother was the best spy in the history of modern times, and she trained you from childhood, even earlier than her own start. Do you know why Mozart was Mozart? Because he started to learn music from early childhood, soaking it in while his father, an expert himself, taught Nannerl, his older sister. Your early exposure from someone who had early exposure makes you unique."

"Are you forgetting what Tamara said to you? I'm not Molly, Vitali Ignatiy."

"All right, enough of that. You are the only one there is. You are Molly. Try not to agonize over it."

"What am I supposed to agonize over?"

He points to the radio. "The sound you hear is not random or static. It's an amplified signal coming from you."

"What?"

"It only comes from originals, not duplicates."

Swallow. Breathe. Do not panic. "What are you saying?"

"How do you think the duplicates home in on the original? Originals broadcast a signal, and the duplicate receives it. The duplicate follows the signal, or tries to, but does not generate any of its own."

"This is impossible. I'm not Molly, I don't have her scars, and I don't make duplicates when I bleed. Molly is dead."

"Do you mind if one of the tamaras inspects your body?"

"Knock yourself out."

"Might you have got mixed up?"

"No."

"Tell me what you remember about the last time you saw her."

I do. I also take off my top and show him my back. "Molly got bitten by a duplicate once, and the scar on her back was permanent. What do you see?"

"No bite mark."

"I'm not Molly, Vitali Ignatiy, I'm a molly."

"Did Mykhaila teach you chess?"

"Yes. I don't like it."

He laughs. "But you know the rudiments. You can play?"

I nod.

"Okay, from what I know, in all my research, an original has never died before the duplicates. Perhaps there is something in the cell profile that allows promotion."

"A pawn that reaches the other end of the board."

"Becomes a queen. You, Molly, have been promoted to queen."

"But I don't make duplicates."

"No, you don't. Shame." Yet his voice does not sound sorry.

"How do you know so much?"

"I stumbled on the Soviet program while researching infertility. Most of this information was handed to me in Belarus and St. Petersburg. I did not even have to bribe or coerce anyone. They were almost giving me papers like garbage disposal. Nobody cares about classified documents because people are getting out of the crumbling USSR, destroying what is incriminating and discarding everything else casually. I built it up from there."

"You dodged the question before. You knew my mother."

"I met her once, but I knew her on paper better than anyone, yes. She was pregnant with you . . . with Molly. I tracked her down like I did the other participants in the program. Like Tamara."

"My mother, Molly's mother wasn't a participant. She stole it."

"Not exactly. She was an unwitting participant, but a participant all the same, Molly. The people who sent her knew it would come down to injecting herself. Her handlers had orders to inject her if she did not do it herself."

"So, she was a pawn too."

"All spies are pawns, my dear."

"Did she become a queen?"

He pauses, glances at the floor, then back up. "She became a knight."

"Knight. Right. Vitali Ignatiy, what do you want of me?"

"Me? I'm an old conspiracy theorist who hand-prints a newsletter. I want to be heard. I . . . know things. I've seen things, but most of them too fantastical for the general public to believe—"

"Stop. Cut that shit out. I don't buy altruism. Try again, or I'm walking out."

He smiles. "You are just like her. I don't want anything

from you, Molly. I did want to see you, and I'm grateful that you visited. It is, in some ways, like seeing a ghost, but a welcome one. Tamara!"

The tamaras come in.

"It's time to go."

~

On the way back one tamara asks, "Why call him 'Vitali Ignatiy' all the time? Why not just 'Vitali'?"

"Russian naming conventions. It's polite to use what you call the first and middle name."

She nods and keeps driving.

I flip through the sheaf of papers I filched from Niki-tovich's office, but it's too dark in the vehicle, so I slip them under my blouse and into the waistband of my trousers for later. I wish I had James to look at them. I picture him as I had last seen him, gobbling up food, and I pinch myself hard in the inner thighs to get my mind off him.

Transcript

It's getting difficult to breathe. The mass is pushing against my lungs, but also my stomach. I can't eat or drink more than a few sips.

[PD breathes heavily and struggles to speak.]

[cut]

Eight

I read the research material surrounded by phantom mollys, six of them, with accusing eyes and no words. Talking to Nikitovich has tripped up my mindfulness and bruised my ability to ignore them.

Some of the stuff I'm reading is in Russian, but most has been translated. I speak a little Russian and I remember how my mother called me *dorogoy* because she did not want me to consider myself weaker than a male.

What the research shows is that the difference between the primes and the duplicates lies in the spleen, which produces specialized, artificial cells. All those years ago when Mykhaila worked in Russia, she stole and injected herself with a primary suspension of those cells. They nested in her spleen and lay dormant. When she became pregnant with Molly they activated and the child was born with the ability to make blood copies, hemoclones.

I'm surprised to find out Mykhaila had a splenectomy, though there is no information about whether she ever made duplicates. Why else would she have had her spleen taken out? I remember seeing her scar. I imagine the scenario, the army of mykhailas. This may have been why both Connor and Mykhaila Southbourne were so proficient with the rules before Molly was born, and knew exactly what skills their child would need. I break out in a sweat thinking of duplicate mykhailas wandering around the British countryside. She was deadlier than Molly, and if they attack me . . .

The artificial cells act as matter converters. Their design has not been penetrated by any scientists outside the Iron Curtain, but from a drop of blood they can make a full human duplicate based on the genetic material of the Prime from almost any base material: wood, soil, organic waste, even metals.

I have to stop; the more I read, the more intense the ghost mollys become. I wonder what I will find if I take a sample of my spleen and examine it under the microscope. Would the special cells line the splenic channels? Or would they have their own gland budding off like a science-fiction alien? If I return to work I will find a way to biopsy myself.

I can't say when I fall asleep, or at what point the dream begins, but it's always best to just ride it out. I should not have to pay for sins I did not commit. I didn't kill the mollys, so I should not have the nightmares, the shakes, the deep regrets, the ghosts.

I see me. My face, crumpling under my own fist. The mollys don't register pain, even when they are deep in it. They cry out involuntarily, but no rictus or grimace, even while I break their arms or push their shoulders out of joint.

I see myself in dirt, in the mud behind Southbourne Farm, struggling to get my head up, but my arm holding me under, caught on a root system.

They fight, the mollys do. Ferocious, not as polished as me, not yet, but effective. Only, not effective enough. In rubble, in a place I do not recognize, I am on the verge of losing, but I push both thumbs into the molly's eye sockets. It's short work from there.

So many, each one a millstone on my heart.

Then everything stops and there's Molly, my original, my Prime, sitting on a deck chair, legs spread, hands on her knees, serene. The skin over her knuckles is cut up, hanging off in disorganized flaps. She is dirty, like she has been fighting, which of course she has. There is soot on her face and her hair is bedraggled. I'm on the floor, maybe chained, maybe lying on a beach towel, both possibilities equal like they can be in dreams.

"You know, when I first moved to London I used to stare out of the window a lot, at night, at the lights of other people's lives. A part of me expected to see a crime being committed, like in that Hitchcock movie. Nothing ever did happen, but I still expected it." She exhales, shrinks a little.

"You fucked me," I say.

"I gave you a choice."

"Not an informed one. I wasn't twenty-four hours old."

"Boo-hoo. Manage your expectations, girl. This isn't Hitchcock. I didn't get to choose, and neither did my mother. Besides, you still have a choice."

"What do you mean?"

She stands, now holding lighter fluid like she was on the first and last day I met her. "You can choose each day whether or not to be Molly Southbourne."

She douses herself and catches fire, smiling. Flaming, skin blackening and falling off in irregular patches, she leaps to embrace me. From behind her other burning mollys join.

I wake crying, and I cannot stop for thirty minutes, so I punch myself in the temple, twice, hard, so hard that I see stars. A molly watches me from the foot of the bed, head cocked.

I hate this shit.

I should go back on my medication. Again.

I opt for coffee instead. I'm in the kitchen, hand-grinding beans with a rolling pin, and my hopeful eye on a drizzle cake that someone left unattended, when one of the tamaras comes in. She seems overdressed for the hour.

She says, "Some of us are going to the pub. You want to come?"

~

I am at the bar on a stool, facing a mirror, looking at my own reflection and that of an oil painting on the wall behind me. The painting is of two young boys carrying a blindfolded angel on a litter of some sort. There is also the reflection of a television on which Margaret Thatcher is speaking words with great passion. The image switches to that of an ambulance, probably because the army and navy are manning the ambulance service in order to break the strikes. It's amazing that they've decided to televise the House of Commons live. TV is becoming weird.

The others are dancing and intermittently inviting me despite my resolute refusal. For obvious reasons only two of the duplicates are allowed to go out to avoid undue attention, but I notice some have disguised themselves effectively. Tamara doesn't have rules like Molly's, but she has what she calls "advisory tactics." We're not supposed to dance, either, but you try getting any group of young people to obey any rules.

Dancing is good for you, dorogoy. *The great fighter Bruce Lee was also a champion dancer. Did you know that?*

"You like the print?"

I turn. The bartender is staring at me. He's young, sounds like he might be German or Austrian or something. Some darkness about the upper lip, but otherwise clean-shaven.

"It's interesting," I say.

I thought I was off both booze and sex, but by the end of the evening I'm in his bed where he lives above the pub, and I'm slightly buzzed. A naked molly had done somersaults in the air while I fucked the bartender, but now she is gone. I watch him sleep. There is brown fuzz growing up from his arse crack, up his back. He sleeps like a child, with no cares, no thrashing. His name is Wolf and he is a backpacker. He tells me the painting is Finnish, *The Wounded Angel* by Hugo Simberg, 1903.

He gives it to me even though it is not his to give, and in the early hours I walk through the streets like an art thief with the rolled-up painting under my arm and my shoes dangling from my hand.

~

In the intoxicated state, a memory swirls to the top, reminding me of why I should abstain.

Molly is fifteen. She and her parents are in a clearing to the east of the house at Southbourne Farm, and it is one of those balmy August mornings, sunny, warm, but not unpleasant. There is a cow lowing with maternal heartbreak for a dead calf, but Connor is investigating that. A breeze cools their sweaty skin after the morning run, and their breathing calms. Molly senses the tension in her mother, even before Mykhaila speaks.

"I'm sorry, baby."

"For what?" Molly is nervous, because hard as her mother is, she does not usually apologize.

She walks behind a tree and comes back with a blue head guard. "Put this on, Molly."

"Why? I've never worn one when we spar." She straps the Velcro chin strap on. Neither she nor her mother has gloves on, but Molly clenches her fists, raises her guard, places her left foot forward, and waits for her mother's command.

"At ease, Molly. Today, we do something different." Her eyebrows come together and lines appear between them. "I should have completed this part of your training earlier, but I was weak. I . . . don't want to." She takes a deep breath.

"Mum, get on with it. The suspense is killing me more than whatever you'll do."

"You can fight. You're fast and tough and creative with

your combinations. You aren't showy, you do what has to be done efficiently. One aspect of your training, though, is improving your ability to take hits. We haven't done that."

"How do I train for taking hits?"

"By taking hits. Keep your guards down, stand there, and take what I give you."

"Okay. Any advice?"

"Keep loose. Your natural response would be to tense up. Don't. Control your breathing."

"Okay, Mum. I'm read—"

Molly does not see her mother move. Her vision explodes into fireworks, multiple pins of light, and even when she crashes to the ground, there is no pain. Curious. Her vision clears, and Molly sees tears trickling down Mykhaila's face.

It continues, progressing from punches to kicks, and the pain comes soon enough. But you can get used to anything, even a beating, even when each impact forces air out of your lungs and you fear damage is being done to your internal organs, even the possibility of death.

"Now, *dorogoy,* fight, with everything, like you mean to survive. *Go!*"

Molly pours all her combat training into the fight, throwing sand into her mother's eyes, pulling hair when she can, tripping, shoving, biting, and spitting. Mykhaila parries all the attacks, but nods with approval.

When it is over Molly collapses in a heap, notices Connor at the edge of the clearing. Something passes between her parents, a subtle disagreement, perhaps.

When Molly is soaking in a bath and her mother is washing the grime off her back, they both hear the door slam and the car engine start.

Mykhaila starts to sing as the sound becomes fainter.

~

Since the night out the security around me is lax. I suspect the tamaras followed me and waited when I stayed the night at Wolf's. I may have been too drunk to spot them.

The number of mollys around me has increased, and I cannot help reacting to them, which earns me odd looks from the tamaras. I try to escape into sleep, but my dreams are anything but restful. I relive the murders of Molly Southbourne, and I am punished for them.

When I can't take it anymore, and I am afraid I will endanger the tamaras, I leave the house, ostensibly to take a walk. Instead, I go back to West London, knowing they will be watching for me there.

I ride the night bus part of the way, but I walk for the last mile. I have my hat, my bandanna, my Zorro makeup, and my ruffled skirt. I want to be seen. I want to be followed.

One of the tamaras is on my tail. I've known this since I got off the bus, but I haven't done anything about it. It's nice to have backup, but I don't want her to give me away because she does not know my strategy. My destination is the address they told me to report to for testing. I'm trying to decide what to do about the tamara when I spot the first government agent. I'm sure the site is not hot anymore, but they must have considered the possibility that I would be back and left someone to mind the shop.

He probably does not have enough staff to follow me, but I'm guessing he'll be reporting back. This might take time, or he might have one of those mobile phones. I lead him to a place I can double back on. I see the tamara become tentative, and I think she's twigged that I'm doing something, but not what.

On this occasion, London smells fresher to me, like the wind has generated a reprieve from the filth and chemical muck. A dog barks somewhere. I do not miss the tamara following me, but she has not noticed the agent. I double back on myself, confusing her while I hide behind a wheelie bin. When I let her agonize over my location, snapping her head left and right, I tap her shoulder from behind.

"Tamara, why are you here?" I ask.

She starts, but does not look surprised.

"I'm here to help," she says.

"You're . . . I appreciate the effort."

The dog stops barking, I stop talking, the world itself seems to go still. I'm running before I know what's happening and I pull the tamara with me, against all my training. The first shots hit the concrete wall to my left, and I feel splinters on my skin. The tamara has started running on her own steam, so I drop her hand. The reports for the shots vary, so we are dealing with more than one shooter. I change direction and duck behind a car, and across the road, the tamara does the same, hiding in a spot from where she can see me. I have no gun. Never bring a fist to a gunfight.

On cue the tamara reaches into her handbag and slides a gun across to me—an unloaded semiautomatic. She shoves a magazine across just as the firing starts up again. I do not want to wait for ground troops to arrive. I hear sporadic screams and shouts. General people, scared, confused. And there are mollys all around, distorting my sense of the danger. This is a situation from which to retreat. I have no idea who I'm dealing with, and while I know the lay of the land from when I lived in the area, I do not know how many people they have or how well armed they are. The tamara's chest caves in, and before

I can make sense of it her head shatters. Her brain lands two feet away from what's left of her neck stump. High-velocity shot.

I don't hesitate. I run toward a lane that I know will take me out. A shot misses me, but it's close enough that I feel the air displaced. I lose the hat. A part of me knows I'm not going to make it, and I'm strangely calm. Less calm when I see two tamaras running straight for me. Behind me the bullets get closer, while from door-ways, from inside cars, climbing out of windows, dozens of tamaras emerge and converge.

"Get the fuck out of my way," I say.

They don't. Some of them fall under the gunfire, but before I know it the tamaras are scrumming around me. When I'm fully surrounded they lock arms with one an-other and me, tamaras jumping on top of us to form a roof. It is like an ancient Roman infantry defense maneu-ver, like a tortoise. I hear their cries as they die. They all but lift me bodily out of danger and farther into the night. My boots drag along the road. The shots continue and blood drips onto my hair and down my face. Teeth and shattered bone fall like hail in the storm of blood. Body shots result in a rank smell of shit from pierced bowels. I am grazed by one bullet, and I strain my ankle when I attempt to run for myself. When one tamara dies an-other quickly replaces it. *Her.* Replaces her. Their cries are truncated, and there is weeping, but all of this is heard through an adrenaline haze. I cannot tell you what is true and what is imagined, what is tears and what is sweat from fear or exertion. We pass through the dark streets like a carnival of the impossible, trailing blood and dead tamaras.

Nine

Tamara thinks I'm suicidal.

She doesn't say it, but it's in her eyes. She thinks whatever was in my Prime is in me, and that I'm going to kill myself. She thinks I'm a danger to her and wonders if I'm worth saving. This is a rational thought when you're elbow deep in blood. Though there are numerous dead and broken, Tamara says we have to pack up and move because we will be traced. She is saving the conversation with me for later.

Am I suicidal? I don't know. I've certainly been stupid and I can't formulate strategy to save my life. I can't just use memories of what I've been taught. I need experience.

"Southbourne, pick up the pace or get out of the way," says Tamara.

Three tamaras holding weapons stand guard at the periphery of our field hospital. Some are out on the street, keeping watch, and one is specifically tasked with manning the phone, in case someone calls in. The tamaras have field medical training, picked up from somewhere.

I know some first aid, but nothing on this level. Blood transfusions are easy when everybody has the same blood type. There is a quiet hurry, organized, lacking the panic I would expect in this situation. I reinsert myself into the moment, assisting, fetching, discarding, holding hands.

Three transports arrive and take the tamaras off to a new location. I leave with the third, even though Tamara wants me in the first.

The new place is a disused factory. The inside has been modified and I'm sure work must have been done before today. I wonder how many contingency plans Tamara has. I'm too tired and buzzed from adrenaline to decode the symbolism of moving from church to factory. The floor has been divided up by wooden boards, and the windows blacked out. I make myself small, I change bandages, I clean up blood, I take sentry shifts, I anticipate. A fortnight passes and nobody comes for us. Nothing makes the papers, a silence that is loud in and of itself.

Tamara and I go for a walk among the brutal industrial buildings. It's evening, and the area is mostly abandoned, so it's safe. I'm not wearing my Buffalo Gal makeup because it's too distinctive.

"How do you feel about teaching?" she asks. She keeps her eyes straight ahead.

"Teaching what?"

"Everything you know. Anatomy, spycraft, hand-to-hand. Just teach a few of us; we'll teach the others."

"Because you think I might die and the knowledge will be lost?"

"Are you going to die?"

"We all are."

"You know what I mean."

"I'm not going to kill myself, Tamara. At least not today."

"Then you can spend your time teaching."

~

I swear this used to be easier.

My muscles are on fire, my joints are lubricated with acid, and my heart is pumping molten lava. Half a mile left to return to base, yet I want to collapse right here and never get up again. In the final stretch, when I sprint, squeezing yet more energy out of my depleted muscles, I see one of the tamaras waiting for me on the porch of the factory.

I slow and stop in front of her, the original, I think. She has an unaffected confidence that I envy.

"The troops are waiting," she says.

"Thank you." It comes out more formal than I had intended.

A tamara wafts out of the side door, flicks her eyes in my direction, then goes to her original. She cups a hand over her mouth and whispers in Tamara's ear. Her free hand reaches for the tamara's and their hand-holding is intimate, so much that I look away, feeling voyeuristic, like I've seen a private thing. I have no relationship with anyone like that. The tamara goes in without another glance at me.

"There's been a new arrival. I have to go meet her."

My mother's voice comes to me. Molly's mother. *"It."* Not *"her,"* dorogoy. *"It."* Always *"it."*

"How do you do that?"

"Do what?"

"Keep close to them. Keep them close. How do you like each other? They do what you tell them."

Tamara says, "We have a few minutes. Come with me."

Tamara's space is larger than mine, but populated with bunks and mattresses on the floor. There are two tamaras in the room, one lounging on a bed and one standing barefoot, naked, in the center of the room. The one on the floor pipes up, afraid of blame. "Don't say a word. I tried to dress her, but she shrugged the clothes off."

Tamara steps forward and gathers the duplicate into her arms. "Welcome." She sniffs at the hair. "Where did she . . . ?"

"Found her in the garden." They had improvised a garden on the roof.

Tamara whispers something long and convoluted, and the duplicate smiles.

"Let's go," she says.

"Is that it?" I ask.

"It's too bad your mother taught you to kill yours."

"The mollys."

"Perhaps try to love them, instead?"

I train the tamaras, not to any degree that would make them soldiers or spies, but enough to respond to commands and hit back when attacked. Tamara is the most useful, and she probably has more knowledge and the most complete memory. It is a bit difficult getting her to unlearn the techniques she has depended on for so long. I start by refining her reach, changing her choices, improving her flexibility—making her a better her. When she trusts me I introduce what I think might be useful from Systema, then Brazilian jujitsu. It's as complete an education as I can offer with limited time.

At the back of my mind, I know this will make it easier for them to subdue me when we next have a confrontation. It makes no difference to me because I have never been able to overcome Tamara's numbers.

The phantom mollys at first watch with baleful expressions, and a month later begin to copy the actions of the tamaras, as if they themselves are training.

Only a few of them take the anatomy classes, but those who do are very keen. I learn that over the years Tamara and the tamaras have gathered to themselves a vast expertise in a number of subjects by distributed learning. They have nurses, accountants, cooks, surveyors, artists, and a whole raft of middle management tamaras. Tamara is hyperorganized and contingency centered. They have money, they have multiple jobs all over London, and there are properties and bolt-holes ready at a moment's notice. While I teach them, I pick all of this up.

I am hardest on myself, of course. I get fit, and I feel the callus build on my hands, elbows, and feet. In between conditioning, I watch the peaceful duplicates and learn how they love one another.

~

Most nights, I fall into a deep sleep and don't wake until morning. One night, bladder full because of too much caffeine, I rise and on my way to the toilet I hear whispers. This I would have ignored, but it is a man's voice.

". . . relative to her?" says the man.

"Are you kidding? I have never seen anything like her. Combat is a sublime art that she embodies. Her reflexes are phenomenal and her instincts are inhuman. And I mean I think she is a new kind of human. I sometimes imagine that she invented violence and the rest of us are pale imitators. I, we, will never be that good." This is Tamara.

"But you will be good enough?"

I know the voice.

It is Vitali Ignatiy Nikitovich.

This isn't going to work.

    [PD exits.]

    [cut]

Ten

I don't just leave the next morning. I wait for Tamara to bring up the visit, but she doesn't. She acts as if nothing happened. Options tumble in my mind, wondering if what I heard is benign, if I'm overreacting, what other possible explanations there could be, but even though there is much I don't know, the secrecy leaves me feeling unsettled, and unsafe, and a Molly Southbourne who does not feel safe soon erupts into violence. The phantom mollys seem to agree, because about five of them just converge and try to stare me to death. I think hard at them: *Fuck off!*

I escape without killing or maiming anyone. One day I leave for my daily jog and just keep going.

I stuff all my money in my sports bra, put on my jogging gear, and that's it. I don't spend any time agonizing. Luckily we put on partial disguises when leaving the factory anyway, so my efforts to look different are not remarkable to the few tamaras who are awake. The morning comes with a mist that I break through like a zombie. I get catcalled by men on the early shift, and catch stares when I get on the first bus I can find. A part of me thinks the other passengers are working for the government. I disembark after an hour with the dawn sun in my eyes.

My heart hammers in the rib cage much longer than it should, but I am unmolested, for now. I walk calmly away from the bus and change clothes as soon as I find a Salvation Army bin. I select a man's apparel, compress my hair into a woolen hat, and disguise my walk. Nobody approaches me as I spiral farther away from the bus stop on side streets and alleys. When I get tired, I find an alcove where I sit, watching three drunks argue until all the office workers start their perambulations. A sadness comes upon me, but I shrug it off. Sadness is a luxury for later.

I wait outside a supermarket until a shopper in a hurry leaves his car running. I don't drive well, or at all. Molly could, though. I don't think, I just gun the engine and screech out of there. I take the car south, out of the city, have several near misses, and keep going until it runs out of gas around Plumstead. I cross the road, and take buses to random destinations. By nightfall I slip into the harsh scrub of Southmere Park in Thamesmead. I walk over stubby grass, not stopping until I reach the cover of trees, and I'm close enough to civilization that I can get supplies, but far away enough that I can finally rest. Ghost mollys stand guard around me as I sleep.

~

I settle into a routine of sorts, taking my breakfast from the bugs and crawlies under a rock or whatever I can find stripping bark, shitting in holes, washing and drinking from Southmere Lake, exploring for items that might be of use, like stones and rocks of different shapes and sizes. It is cold, but I place dry leaves and moss between layers of clothing as insulation, a skill Molly learned from a homeless man. I can't find any pyrite, but I have made a stone ax, a knife, and a hand mill. *Neolithic human, bitches,* I say to the phantoms. I initially plan to use the lake as a food source, for both fish and invertebrates, but I have to be careful of campers and the Southmere is not exactly teeming with life.

While I'm living in the wild, I have time to reflect, and keep coming back to the same problem. What was Vitali plotting with Tamara? The first Molly's memories come to me in irregular bursts, although I have a lot of her knowledge. I am sure that until Tamara introduced me I had never met Vitali.

I meditate. Nothing fancy, just panic control and significance mining. In those cold, dark nights I decide I want to live, to survive. I decide to be Molly Southbourne and to stop playing at being her. Me. Up until now I have been drifting, following the currents that come my way, but that's not how I was taught.

At night I make forays to the nearby areas, stealing what I need, paying for others if I think I will not be remembered. I take stray bits of clothing, some utensils, matches, food, sanitary pads, alcohol, infrequently enough that they might be considered misplaced, not stolen. From a distance I hear their music, their copulations, their arguments, and I smell their hash. Not so neolithic anymore.

I'm scraping edible lichen off a rock one morning when I hear movement behind me. I already know it's too late before I turn. The police are all around me, beyond striking distance. My weapons are at my base, and all I have with me is my stone knife and my two giant ovaries. They have semiautomatic weapons, drawn, and with the kind of commitment in their eyes that tells me to surrender. But I wake up and I'm surrounded not by cops, but by phantom mollys and the sound of rain battering my shelter. Even in the gloom I can see the whites of their eyes and they remind me of a statue of Medusa I once saw, frozen in a silent scream.

I talk to the mollys and I am not alarmed when they start talking back at me. I accept that I am occasionally psychotic, and I accept that I need medication, maybe all the time, maybe not, but at this stage of my short life, talking makes me calmer.

"We can't keep running," I say.

The molly I'm talking to agrees. "We need a place to live, to settle, before we catch our death out here."

"Mother taught us how to live rough," I say. "I picked up a lot from Tamara, I know what to do, but we have more urgent matters to deal with first. We need to make ourselves safe."

"How?"

"We need to take the fight to those who want to harm us."

"No more running?" says the molly.

"No more running," I say.

"I like this plan," she says.

~

I start by calling the tattoo number from a phone box in Abbey Wood Station.

"The number you have dialed has not been recognized. Please hang up and dial again. The number you have dialed has not been recognized. Please hang up and dial again. The number you have dialed has not been recognized. Please hang up and dial again."

I hang up.

My calls have always gone through before, and I don't know what this means.

I try one more time with the same result. It's interesting the kind of sinking feeling you get when the foundations of your world are shaken. Without the voice on the other end of the phone, I am without options. I don't quite hear a voice, but I get a strong impression of my mother's disapproval. She would no doubt say she raised me to always have options. But that wasn't me; that was Molly. I am an imperfect copy, a fraud. Like the goldcrest I saw. In legend, they're called the "king of birds," but it's said they hid in the feathers of an eagle and, using it as a launchpad, soared higher to be crowned. I'm hiding in Molly's feathers, but I won't get crowned, I won't become a queen or a knight.

Since I can't get through, I'm left with two options, but I'm not going to Tamara's tamara factory, where she and her mass-produced army will be ready for me. Instead, I find my way back to Vitali's house. The ghost mollys and I watch it for ten days and take notes on his comings and goings.

"Should we go in and look around while he's away?" asks the nearest ghost.

I shake my head. "Not enough information. Too risky."

"So we search, get more information, and make it less risky," she says. "We need to know what we're dealing with."

"What if we can't lock the doors after breaking in?"

"Then we make it look like a robbery," she says.

Breaking into places is not as easy anymore as it was in my mother's day. Technology has advanced way beyond her imagining. Pressure-sensitive sensors, motion detectors, infrared cameras, temperature-activated tear gas. Some of what she taught me is still relevant. Patience, watching people, getting as much information as I can before attempting to break in, expecting anything once the door is open. Compared to all of this, Vitali's place is uncomplicated, probably because he doesn't expect us, or anyone. It's relatively straightforward to get in.

It's a two-story building and we don't find anything unexpected on the ground and top floors. The office is the same as when I last saw it. Then I remember the noises and his basement printing press.

The ghost mollys find a door beneath the staircase, and I find the key in the back of his precious picture frame. The lock looks old, and I expect to have to jiggle around, but the key slides home like it's planing on oil. The stairwell that descends from the door is narrow, even for me, and I can't imagine how Vitali manages. It's dark, although there's a glow from the basement landing. No handrail, and I have to guide myself with the walls. At the bottom the level opens into a single wide space lit with fluorescent tubes. I blink from the change in illumination, but I still can't quite believe what I'm seeing.

Two mollys, alive, with severe burn scars and caged like animals. Two tamaras leap from the chairs they lounged on, intent on stopping me. They are talking, but all I can hear is the blood singing in my ears. They're unprepared, and are more like caregivers than guards. I weave in and out of their swings, assessing their skill first, then striking back, straight midsection kicks that send them both to the floor.

I'm so taken by the sight of the mollys that neutralizing the tamaras is automatic, lizard-brain activity. I tie the tamaras up without breaking a sweat.

Two mollys, alive, in Vitali's basement. I was here. *I was here* and I didn't feel them. I walk toward the cages in a trance. They do not react to me, or to the violence I do to their guards. Maybe drugged. One does not have a left eyelid, and that side of her face and cranium is smooth, hairless, skin all corrugated. Tears flow from that eye in a steady stream that she does not wipe away. The second has a withered hand and leans to one side like she's had a stroke.

I reach out through the bars, with both hands.

"Hello. You are safe with us, with me," I say. I don't know if they can see the phantoms. Probably not.

I embrace them both the way I have seen Tamara do with her own duplicates, the cold of the bars pressing against me as I press against them. A part of me isn't sure this will work; a part of me just believes mollys are evil and violent, and no Kumbaya can change that, but I am determined that I will never kill another molly.

I whisper in their ears, "I love you. I will always fight for you, not against you."

"Hey! You never told me you loved me," says one of the ghosts.

"I love you, Molly-in-My-Mind."

"Good. Let's free our sisters and get the fuck out of here."

"I like this plan," I say.

But there's more beyond the cages, vast numbers of boxes and filing cabinets, all full of information about me and Tamara and others like us, watched, "culled," kept safe, employed. I read as much as I can, but it's too much, and I've already dawdled too long. I'm not leaving this information here, and I can't take it with me. My life started with fire.

I take a trip to the kitchen. . . .

~

I can't take the burned mollys to live in the bush with me. If I did, they would cope, but they have a shell-shocked feel to them. I need more.

I don't feel sorry for myself, my mother trained me for

worse, but I do realize I can't exist like this. I think of Southbourne Farm and discard it instantly. That's where Tamara picked up my trail, and the government would clearly be watching it at least intermittently.

I need someone who might still care for me.

~

I have to seek out James Down. We did not part on the best of terms: he ended things with a letter and lab results showing a molly cocoon growing within his abdomen. The last time I saw him was just before I went into the mental hospital, back at the university, where he was feeding like a caterpillar.

He still lives in the house I remember where we fucked and fought at times. His car is in the driveway, and lights come on at night, so I know someone's home. I survey the neighborhood for three days, but it doesn't seem to me like it's being watched.

All the phantom mollys disappear when I near the house. I do not know what this means. I make the burned mollys stand guard outside. I ask them nicely.

Close up I can observe the layers of filth on the car, like it hasn't been wiped down in a long time. There is nothing in the rubbish bin. A few charity appeal pamphlets are scattered around the front door. The garden has gone back to bush. I creep around to the back door and find it ajar.

Stench. Not of death, but of neglect, which is consistent with the outside of the property. Dust everywhere. Every surface has discarded food containers. I can hear the hiss of an untuned radio or something similar. I have to pick my way carefully, because sharp edges of broken bottles and opened sardine cans litter the floor.

"James?" I say. "Are you in here?"

The carpet looks like mud, water damage, and dirt matting the fibers together.

There are marks on the ceiling, watermarks that show splash patterns. The walls are covered in similar stains, some wet. Impact, then dripping down. I stop to examine a patch. It looks like vomit. Smells like it too.

"James, it's Molly Southbourne. Hello?"

I think I hear a voice from upstairs, so I go that way. I've been there before, naked, kissing James, giggling, slipping down when distracted by his ministrations. We made love on this very staircase once or twice. In addition to the radio, the TV is on, so I switch it off before going up. I steal up the steps. I have to hold my nose now because the smell intensifies. It is now more feculent and . . . fresh, rather than stale.

"James?"

". . . here . . ." His voice comes from his bedroom.

I hesitate briefly, then I push the door with my foot.

Before I see anything I choke on the intensity of the smell of wrongness and rot. The room is dark, a bedside lamp struggling valiantly. All I can see of James is a distended belly, larger than the rest of him, about six feet in diameter, tight as a drum, reticulate with veins. The skin is thin as a teenager's pimple. James twitches feebly at the side of this tumorous mass. His arms and legs are like twigs with crumpled skin, and his rib cage appears tiny, spread at the bottom to make way for the belly. He is naked, but his genitals are shrunken and soaked in a pool of piss and excrement.

"...Molly..."

A change comes over the mass. There is movement under the skin of the bulge, in multiple places. James's mouth opens in a silent scream. His tongue flicks out, dry and pink, ineffective. I am frozen to the spot, trying not to breathe, upset that there are no phantom mollys to block my view.

The skin on James's belly points and ruptures. Straw-colored fluid sprays outward in all directions, pressure relieved, and I am drenched in it. A molly pulls herself free, hair plastered to her skull, blinking away blood so she can see, scrambling toward me. I recoil, slip, and fall into the muck. She follows and is on me. The shock of physical contact paralyzes me—a part of me thought her a phantom until that moment. She slams my head into the floor, which wakes me out of my trance.

As my head spins and my vision blurs, all my instincts and training tell me to use deadly force, yet my time with Tamara makes me hesitate. Despite all Molly Southbourne's sins, *I* have never killed my own duplicates. Is now the time to start? My mother's voice bubbles up with lethal combat advice, and I tamp it right down again. I force my yammering nerves to calm.

With the slipperiness and the fact that this is a molly, a furious creature that wants to kill me, I have a harder time than Tamara subduing my copy. The molly shows no restraint, and comes at me with everything she has. I dodge, parry, take some hits, looking for an opportunity. She never backs down, never flags, and to calm her I have to break her right forearm and dislocate her left shoulder. I am about to break her knees when she goes limp from the pain. I collapse beside her. I feel a flood of gratitude that I did not have to kill, and I burst into tears, hacking sobs that come from a deep well of sorrow and loneliness.

I check on James—he is still, dead. I put gentle pressure on his neck, but the carotid is now quiet. I killed him, just like he said.

I tie up the molly with strips of curtain, feeling intense déjà vu for what Molly Prime did to me, and I strip off, then enter the shower. I wash with the door open so I can keep an eye on the molly.

She is awake by the time I'm done.

~

"Hyperalimentation," says James.

He recorded some videos before he died and I am watching them with one eye on the molly. She's gone still, not wasting energy on unyielding bonds.

"Let's say Molly is sixty, seventy kilos. If I put on that amount of weight, and don't destroy my heart with the strain, the cocoon inside me will have enough mass to build a molly, and leave enough of me to survive. Theoretically."

Oh, James.

I find medical records that show he was assessed by a surgeon. The mass had vascularized, diverted the aorta, and the surgeon had no confidence of removing it without killing James.

He continues talking on the screen, unshaven and gaunt. The video shows some snow on the bottom, needs tracking, but it doesn't matter. He had bigger problems.

"I may have miscalculated," he says in the last video. His skin is papery, streaked with black veins. The whites of his eyes are green and ringed with capillaries. "I didn't factor in that as the mass grows, my ability to keep food down reduces. Everything I eat jets out of me like I'm possessed. If I can't maintain the hyperalimentation, I can't create the bulk. I—"

The image stops there and I can't find any more tapes. Poor James.

I turn to the molly. "Can you talk yet?"

"Yes."

"You know what you are and who I am?"

"When are you from? You have more of her in you, like you're older than me," she says.

"Not by much, a few days at most."

"Are you going to kill me? I have memories of the others you killed. I know how it goes."

"I'm not going to kill you." But I don't know that to be true. I don't know if she will ever relax around me.

"I don't believe you."

I hear Molly Prime's voice: *You don't have to believe my story, but you do have to remember.*

You guys don't all behave the same. You're the eleventh one I've tied up and tried to reason with like this. It didn't end well for the other ten.

I crouch in front of the molly. "I don't want to fight you. I want to tell you a story. Afterwards, I'm going to release you."

"Death can be a release," she says in my voice, with a thought that I had when I was in her shoes.

"Just listen, okay? The story starts with me holding a telephone and watching a house burn. . . ."

Eleven

We go south, four hemoclones looking for a new and peaceful life, settling into new names: me, Mollyann, Moya, and Molina.

I'd like to say we lived rough for a while, but this place is so beautiful that it would give lie to that truth. There is game, there is fertile soil, there is solitude, which is all we need.

It's sunny. We both look beaten up, but Molina's right arm is in a cast, her left in a sling. She got the worst of it. We're both wearing sunglasses, but she has short hair because I cut it.

She hates the name Molina, hates being derivative. Tough shit. I know what's going on in her head, she feels like a molly, and the self-preservation instinct is strong. All she knows is that to survive, she has to kill me. I've confused her by telling her why that's not so. Molina is less feral, less angry, with each passing day, becoming, in spite of herself, more like Molly Prime. I have found her quite libidinous, having walked in on her at the wrong moments. She is not shy about it, and thinks we're the same, which we kind of are. I've grown fond of her.

I leave the three mollys safe and phone Tamara's factory. It goes straight to voice mail.

"You know who this is. You also know by now that I know all of your plans and I want no part of them. If you let this go, I will, and we can all get what we want. If you try to follow me or impede me in any way, I promise you, I will murder you all. Test me, and see."

When I hang up the phone, I feel her watching me, feel the hate behind her eyes.

"Molina, we're family now. We have to look after each other."

She grunts. "You want to be Molly. You feel remorse for James Down. I remember the time he and Molly spent the night fucking one of our kind, killing her in the morning after, so excuse me if I don't feel bad that he's dead."

I remember that too, but I say nothing about it. She's not wrong.

"I was inside him. Do you know how disgusting that feels?"

"I was there, remember?"

"You were not inside someone's abdomen, so don't try to equate our experiences."

"Why did you come out when you did?"

"I felt you. It was intense. I wanted to kill you, like you were Molly."

"I'm not her, though."

"You're trying to be her," says Molina, exasperated. "To be Molly Southbourne. You can't. You'll always be a molly. Stop trying to be something, someone, you're not. Be yourself, be true to your self."

"I don't know who that is," I say.

"Dude, find out. That's what I'm doing. Jesus, do you know how hard it is to wake up every day and not murder you? Your face is the visage of everything I hate, everything I have to defeat in order to survive. If I can overcome that daily, you can overcome your fixation with Molly Southbourne."

"All right, I get that. I can work on that."

"What about them?" She juts her chin toward the burned mollys, Moya and Mollyann, who tend to be quiet and look inward. I swear they are seeing things, like I did. My phantoms have gone for good, and a part of me suspects it was Molina drawing me to her.

"They're our family too," I say.

~

We go into town in Exeter, and we do odd jobs and occasionally steal until we have enough money and forged documents to rent a house. It is a bright and cold spring day when all four of us arrive at the cottage in Dorset. The city is in decline: the young have gone to London for work and excitement, the older folk are quietly dying of beautiful landscape poisoning. It's the perfect place to hide.

I'm in my Buffalo Gal guise again. Molina wears men's clothes, while Mollyann is more traditionally feminine and wears her hair pulled back. The two of them hold hands and wait a few paces behind me. Moya is in the car under blankets, hiding her burns from us and everyone.

The estate agent meets us at the small green gate that breaks the picket. She is smiling, though puzzled.

"Triplets?" she says. She gathers me into the folds of her clothes in a hug. She smells of rosemary and love. I've met her only three times. This must be how they do leasing in the south.

I shrug. "Kind of."

"Are they simple?" She cranes her neck over me to the girls. They are silent.

"Quite the opposite," I say. "Well, except maybe the frizzy-haired one."

"I heard that," says Molina.

We settle in, the four of us. I run a self-defense place in Exeter and I use what I've learned from Tamara to manage our finances and our lives.

I write now. It seems to help me, having all of this out of my head and on paper, like the weight of it no longer pulls me down, like I've exorcised my demons.

I cut away the tattoo on my forearm.

I change my name too. Molly Southbourne is finally dead, and Molina approves.

My new name? No.

I'd have to kill you.

Acknowledgments

The two most important people in the shaping of this book once I created the protoplasm are Aliette De Bodard and Camille Lofters.

A whole bunch of others were instrumental in ensuring that I didn't give up when the Weasels of Doubt came calling: Kate Elliot, Zen Cho, Likhain, Liz Williams, Cindy Pon, Victor Ocampo, Vida Cruz, Alessa Hinlo, Jide Afolabi.

Thanks to Mr. Tom Ilube for being a patron of the (African) speculative fiction arts and funder of the Nommo Awards.

Thanks to the fans who bought and reviewed the first Molly Southbourne book, without whom we wouldn't even be talking about a second book!

Finally, Mission Control: my family (Beth, Cillian, Hunter, David); my agent, Alexander Cochran; my editor, Carl Engle-Laird.

To anyone I might have forgotten, sorry! I'll catch you next time.

About the Author

Carla Roadnight

TADE THOMPSON lives and works in the south of England. He is the author of *The Murders of Molly Southbourne, Rosewater, The Rosewater Insurrection,* and *Making Wolf.* He is a multiple winner of the Nommo Award, winner of the Golden Tentacle Award at the Kitschies, a John W. Campbell Memorial Award finalist, a Shirley Jackson Award finalist, and a nominee for both the British Fantasy Award and the British Science Fiction Association Award. His background is in medicine, psychiatry, and social anthropology. His hobbies include jazz, visual arts, martial arts, comics, and pretending he will ever finish his TBR stack.

TOR·COM

Science fiction. Fantasy. The universe.

And related subjects.

*

More than just a publisher's website, *Tor.com*
is a venue for **original fiction, comics,** and
discussion of the entire field of SF and fantasy,
in all media and from all sources. Visit our site
today—and join the conversation yourself.